NORTHEASTERN ILLINOIS UNIVERSITY

3 1224 00557 2333

W9-AAD-847

Chachaji's Cup

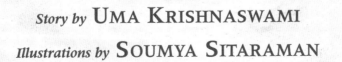

Story *by* UMA KRISHNASWAMI

Illustrations *by* SOUMYA SITARAMAN

CHILDREN'S BOOK PRESS • SAN FRANCISCO, CALIFORNIA

WHEN cups clinked in the kitchen and the water rolled to a boil, everyone in my family knew it was teatime. I set the table. My parents took care of the tea leaves. But as long as he'd lived with us (and that was as long as I could remember), it was Chachaji, my father's old uncle, who was in charge of teatime.

"Plain tea today, Neel?" he'd ask me. "Or shall we have *masala chai*?" And cloves and nutmeg flavors would sing along with the boiling water.

My friend Daniel often came to tea at our house. He loved the cucumber sandwiches Mom made, and the crisp little cookies from the Indian store. Chachaji called them "biscuits."

Chachaji would tip food onto our plates, and milk into our cups. He'd pour in just enough tea to make the spice flavors dance in our mouths. Then, as we all ate and talked, he'd sip slowly and noisily from his old china teacup. Its white surface was creamy smooth, with a spray of pink roses. Its faded gold trim was chipped in spots. It was the only teacup Chachaji ever drank from.

Once I forgot and brought him another cup. "No, *beta*," he told me, "that's the wrong one."

"You really love that old cup," I said to him.

"Old cup for an old man," said Chachaji. And he slurped his tea as the steam rose in little curly waves about his silver head.

"It was his mother's," Mom told me, "your great-grandmother's."

After tea, Daniel
and I often built castles
and forts under the deck,
using sticks and stones
and blocks. Chachaji sat
on the deck and watched us.
Sometimes he came down
and helped us raise a bridge
or topple an enemy's defenses.
When our mothers finally called
us in for homework or baths or
bedtime, he was as sorry as we were.

Chachaji liked to watch old Hindi movies on video tapes rented from the Indian store. They were loud and funny. Daniel and I watched with him. As each scene unfolded, wilder and louder than the last, Chachaji tried to explain it to us. But he laughed so hard he couldn't finish, so in the end we just giggled along.

Chachaji told us stories. He told us about gods and demons. "The great monkey god Hanuman picked up the mountain," he'd thunder, and there it would be, hanging in the air, a whole mountain. "Imagine. He carried the whole mountain."

He told us about his days in the Indian Army. "We marched across the pass," he whispered, "and it began to snow."

And the air would grow chilly in the living room, even in the middle of summer.

Once Chachaji told me about the time when India was split in two. He was just a boy then. "The country was broken," he said. "Suddenly we were two countries. Just like that, India and Pakistan. We had to leave our home. We were refugees, millions of us, on both sides of the border."

I listened openmouthed.

"We walked and walked, for hours," he said. "We took what we could carry with us." And he sipped his tea noisily from the old chipped cup. I looked at him, and I could see the line of people walking.

"Why didn't you take a train, or a plane?" I asked.

Chachaji's eyes were far away. "We had to walk twenty miles, to a place where a car was waiting to bring us across the border to India," he said. "We were lucky. Many people walked all the way, hundreds of miles."

I thought about it. Hiking just two miles with Dad was hard work. How would twenty feel, or a hundred, every step weighed down with sadness?

"This teacup," said Chachaji, "my mother brought it with her at that time, in 1947." His voice grew whispery. "So many things we left behind, but she would not leave that cup."

I looked at the only photograph we had of my great-grand-mother. She seemed far away, in her place on the wall with the other people in my family.

"Everyone laughed at her for taking a breakable thing like a teacup," said Chachaji, "instead of something useful."

What would I take, I wondered, if I had to leave home like that? It was unthinkable.

"She only smiled," Chachaji said. "She knew—if this teacup got to India without breaking, she would get to India without breaking."

I almost didn't dare ask. "Did she?"

Chachaji laughed. "What do you think? Is that her cup? And is it broken?"

"Yes," I said. "No." We laughed together.

The year passed. I grew taller. I could stand on tiptoe and reach things I couldn't before. Daniel was still my very best friend, and he still came over for tea sometimes. But afterwards we went out and shot hoops in the backyard. Chachaji watched from the window, but there were no forts to build anymore, no bridges to raise.

Sometimes we played computer games. "I am too old for computers," said Chachaji.

"That's what my grandma said," said Daniel, "but we got her one anyway and now she has e-mail!" Chachaji smiled and waved us away. "Go play, go play."

At my birthday party that year, Chachaji sat with us and ate cake and ice cream. Mom passed plates of spicy *samosa* and a bowl of fried *gulab jamun* in sweet syrup.

When I blew out all of the candles at once, Chachaji laughed so hard that it set him coughing. Later he started telling us about birthday parties back in India when he was young. But after awhile his story faded, because people began talking about other things.

And when he slurped his tea from the old china teacup, it suddenly sounded far too loud.

That night, it was my turn to wash the dishes. Washing them, I thought of other things, like the camping trip Daniel and I wanted to go on, and the weekend's basketball game. My hands grew slippery with soap. My thoughts scattered.

That was when it happened. The cup fell through my fingers and crashed upon the floor. Its pink roses splintered into a dozen sharp pieces.

"Oh, Chachaji!" I cried." I'm sorry!"

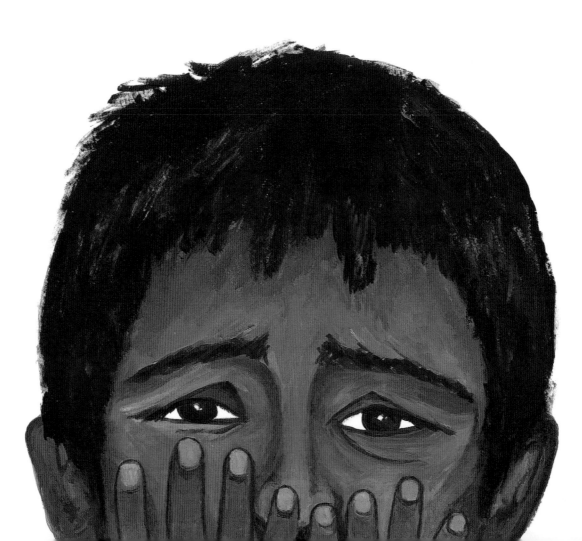

There was a long and terrible silence.

In my mind, I saw a woman walking twenty miles to safety with her son. She held a china teacup as carefully as you'd hold a baby.

The image faded.

We gathered the pieces of the cup. We put them in a paper bag. Chachaji tucked the bag into a closet shelf in his room.

The next week, Dad had to take Chachaji to the hospital. "It's his heart," Dad said. "They need to run some tests. It's not the first time he's had trouble with his heart."

When we went to see him, Chachaji was a small brown ghost against enormous fluffy hospital pillows. He didn't smile.

He didn't smile the next time we went either. Or the next, even though I did my best. I clowned and joked. I twisted my hands into knots and crossed my eyes. All that did was make the nurse frown.

The night before we brought him home, I couldn't sleep. I tossed about, and dreamed of people becoming refugees, leaving their homes. In my dream they walked for miles, fleeing with only the things they could carry. The lines they made crossed the wide plains, from west to east, from east to west. Some hurried to catch cars and trains that waited to take them clear across the land. Only numbers gave them safety. Only hope gave them strength.

I saw Chachaji, young and afraid. I saw his mother, my great-grandmother, her fingers curled around that teacup with roses.

In the early morning, before even the sun was up, I tumbled awake. Where it came from, I don't know, but an idea burned inside me as bright as the promise of sunrise.

I knew what I had to do. I crept to Chachaji's room, and searched in his closet, struggling to keep my rummaging quiet. I tiptoed back to my room.

I lost track of time. When I finally got into bed, the clock was flashing its way toward morning. My fingers were sticky and tired. A small fat package sat wrapped in brown paper upon my desk.

The following afternoon, we wheeled Chachaji down bleach-scented hospital hallways and outside into the sunshine. Before we all loaded in to the car, I leaned over and slipped him the fat brown paper package.

Chachaji frowned. He pulled the bag open. Slowly he lifted out the chipped yellow cup. He peered at the glue smudges blurring the broken roses.

"Thank you," he whispered. "Thank you, *beta*."

"What?" my father asked. "What did you say, Chachaji?"

"Nothing." Chachaji smiled. "Let's go home."

29

When we got home, I said, "Chachaji, it's teatime."

My parents took care of the water and tea leaves the way they always did. Chachaji sat with his hands folded and watched us bustle about the kitchen. I set out cups and plates for everyone. I placed a cup in front of Chachaji, a plain blue one from our plain blue set. From somewhere, like magic, Mom produced a plate of cookies. "My favorite biscuits!" Chachaji exclaimed.

As we sipped tea and ate, our eyes turned to the mantelpiece, We'd made room there for a cup that had traveled long and far. It wasn't much good for holding tea anymore. But I figured you don't have to be shiny new to hold memories.

In 1947, after many years of resistance, India gained its independence from Britain. Until that time, two different religious groups—Muslims and Hindus—had lived together for hundreds of years. With the end of British rule, new borders were drawn and what had at one time been India suddenly became two different countries. One was India, whose people were mostly Hindu. The other country was Pakistan, meant be a homeland for the region's Muslims. This division of India was called the Partition.

Chaos followed the partition of India. Suddenly, many Hindus in Pakistan, and many Muslims in India, felt unsafe where they had made their homes for generations. Over twelve million people fled their towns and villages to cross the border into their newly designated homeland. Never before or since have so many people uprooted themselves to new homes and countries in such a short time.

There is no memorial, no monument to the Partition. For many families, like Chachaji's, only memories remain.

—Uma Krishnaswami

Uma Krishnaswami grew up in India. She is an award-winning author of several children's books, as well as a book for teachers. Her short stories and poems have been featured in multi-author anthologies and in magazines for children. Uma lives with her husband and son in northwestern New Mexico.

To my mother, from whom I learned about the partition of India. —U.K.

Soumya Sitaraman began to paint early in life, with fingerpaints. She developed her unique style in California, where she also curated a multi-artist, mixed media project, Lifelines. Her vibrant paintings reflect elements of Shivite artistry and nature. She currently lives in Bangalore, India.

To my sweetheart Maithreya, I love you best in the world. To Mom and Dad for nurturing the gift; to Aravind for consistent love, support, and understanding; and to Appa and Amma. —S.S.

Library of Congress Cataloging-in-Publication Data

Krishnaswami, Uma, 1956-
  Chachaji's cup / story by Uma Krishnaswami ; illustrations by Soumya Sitaraman.
    p. cm.
Summary: A boy learns about his family history and the Partition of India from his great uncle, through stories told over a beloved old teacup.
  ISBN 0-89239-178-2
  [1. Great-uncles—Fiction. 2. East Indian American—Fiction.]
I. Sitaraman, Soumya, ill. II. Title.
  PZ7.K8978 Ch 2003
  [E]—dc21
        2002006354

01-13-04

Children's Book Press is a nonprofit publisher of multicultural literature for children, supported in part by grants from the California Arts Council. Write us for a complimentary catalog: Children's Book Press, 2211 Mission Street, San Francisco, CA 94110 (415) 821-3080. Visit our website: www.childrensbookpress.org

Story copyright © 2003 by Uma Krishnaswami
Illustrations copyright © 2003 by Soumya Sitaraman

Editors: Ina Cumpiano, Dana Goldberg
Design & Production: Katherine Tillotson
Special thanks to Labony Chakraborty, and to the entire staff of Children's Book Press.

Distributed to the book trade by Publishers Group West. Quantity discounts available through the publisher for educational and nonprofit use.

Printed in Hong Kong through Marwin Productions.
10 9 8 7 6 5 4 3 2 1

Ronald Williams Library
Northeastern Illinois University